C000151203

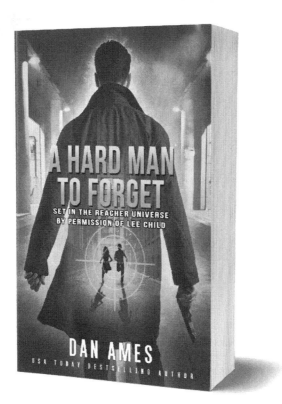

A HARD MAN
TO FORGET

SET IN THE REACHER UNIVERSE
BY PERMISSION OF LEE CHILD

DAN AMES

USA TODAY BESTSELLING AUTHOR

THE JACK REACHER CASES (THE MAN WHO WALKS AWAY)

DAN AMES

FREE BOOKS AND MORE

Would you like a FREE copy
of my story BULLET RIVER and the chance
to win a free Kindle?

Then sign up for the DAN AMES BOOK CLUB:

THE JACK REACHER CASES

(THE MAN WHO WALKS AWAY)

BY

DAN AMES

1

They approached the abandoned farmhouse just
before dawn.

Dawkins went left, to the rear of the structure.
Blatch went right, flanking the target.

Which left the team's leader, Nash, front and center.

A cool, chilling breeze slipped down from the mountains and somewhere a hawk called out.

Nash gathered himself, brought his mind into the kind
of hyper focus required by the battlefield. It was his team,
his mission, his tactics. If they failed, it would be his respon-
sibility. If any of his team didn't make it out, it would be a
burden he would have to shoulder for the rest of his life.

And he had no intention of emerging from the operation
with anything but resounding success.

With the rest of the team in place, Nash approached the
house's front door, not running, but moving swiftly without
making a single sound. He had moved slightly to his right
and stayed low, making him practically invisible from any
viewpoint within the building.

Not that anyone was watching.

Nash and his men had put the enemy force under surveillance for the past week and knew that they'd gotten sloppy, neglecting to set up perimeter security, even going so far as failing to secure the doors and windows.

They'd gotten complacent.

Felt safe.

Overconfident.

That was all about to change, Nash thought.

He kicked in the door and leveled his weapon at the building's occupants, who erupted in a state of panicked, sleepy confusion.

At the same time, Dawkins barreled through the back door, his weapon also aimed at the group who realized they were caught in the worst possible way.

"No!" the enemy's leader shouted at Nash. "Please."

Nash saw unbridled panic in the man's eyes. He couldn't help but feel disappointment. He preferred adversaries who were brave, who put up a good resistance. The fact that he was facing a cowardly enemy made Nash feel the mission was somehow diminished, not exactly a waste of time, but not something he would describe with pride one day to his grandchildren.

"Shut up," he said.

The man begin to blubber, almost incoherent.

"He said to shut your mouth," Dawkins boomed from the back of the room. Nash glanced at him. Dawkins could be a little difficult to control at times. The man had seen the worst of the worst overseas, especially in the caves of Afghanistan and Nash knew he could easily come unhinged. But as the team's leader, it was his job to keep Dawkins in check.

Behind him, he heard footsteps and knew that Blatch had entered the structure as well. No one had attempted to flee.

So far, so good, he thought.

"I have good news and bad news," Nash said to his new captives. "The good news is, if you cooperate, you'll be transferred to a military prison, do some time, and eventually be released back to your own country. The bad news is, if you don't cooperate, you won't be going anywhere."

"Please," the man said again. He was dark-skinned and stocky. Behind him were three more enemy combatants, none of whom were saying a word. They hadn't even tried to reach for their weapons.

Cowards, Nash thought.

"All we want to know is when Zotz will be arriving, and where," he said. "Tell us that, and everything will be fine."

"Who?" the man asked. "I don't know this person you call Zotz."

Nash sighed.

"Answer the question, you son of a bitch," Dawkins boomed. Nash looked at him and saw rage on the big black man's face. Nash quickly realized he had to take control and move quickly. Dawkins pulled a knife from a sheath on his belt. It was a huge blade and Nash knew it was razor sharp.

"Tell us when and where you're planning to make contact with Zotz. Zotz is who we want," Nash said, his voice calm and under control. To his right, Blatch quietly stepped into view, a .45 automatic in his hand.

"Tell them," a shrill voice shouted from behind the man facing Nash.

It was a female.

A woman's voice.

Oh no, Nash thought. From the corner of his eye, he saw Blatch step forward, eagerness in his eyes.

As dangerous and prone to unhinged violence as Dawkins was, Blatch could be worse.

Much worse.

But only when women were involved. Nash had never seen anything firsthand, but there were rumors about Blatch and female combatants. The kind of rumors that were whispered only when neither Blatch, or anyone in charge, was around.

Nash knew he was about to enter some very dangerous territory.

The woman stood up and things went from bad to worse.

Because she was strikingly beautiful, with a lean body, large breasts and long, black hair.

"Hello," Blatch said, a grin on his face. "Jackpot."

Recognition dawned upon the enemy leader and he made a break for the door but Dawkins had seen the move coming and was on the man before he'd taken more than two steps. Dawkins raked the long blade across the man's throat and blood geysered onto the wall. Dawkins rode him to the ground and thrust the enormous knife into the man's body over and over and over again.

Just as quickly, Blatch was on top of the woman, ripping her blouse with one hand, choking her with the other. Blatch dragged her from the room, through the back door, outside.

He wanted privacy to unleash his darkest fantasies on the woman under his control. Nash knew the mission had gone to hell. They weren't going to get any information on Zotz.

But they also couldn't leave any witnesses.

Nash had no choice but to raise his weapon and fire into the forms of the two other enemy combatants, who were sitting, unarmed, with blank expressions on their faces. They were much younger than the man and the woman, but it didn't matter to Nash.

Oh well, he thought. *I tried.*

L auren Pauling stared at the number of zeroes in her bank account.

She had never been a greedy person, never been one to place more emphasis on material belongings than on the truly important things in life. Friends, family, inner peace and happiness.

At the same time, it was a shock to realize she was now a fairly wealthy woman.

When she had decided to sell her private investigative firm to a large corporate competitor, she'd done her homework. Pauling already had a financial advisor, but she'd added a few more professionals to her personal finance team. Now, even after they'd taken the one large sum and broken it up into several different chunks to make the tax hit less severe, Pauling found it hard to believe the accounts were hers.

There was a regular checking account with more money than she could spend in years. There were also various investment accounts holding stocks, bonds, money markets and CDs.

There were also a whole host of other investment vehicles, including an account for real estate acquisition, which she intended to use in the next year or two.

For now, she would keep her co-op in Manhattan, but a country house somewhere, maybe Italy or France, was something she might be interested in.

Patience, she told herself.

Pauling reminded herself of data showing that most lottery winners go on to regret winning – that their lives were far worse after they'd gotten the money.

Pauling knew the comparison wasn't a good one. She'd worked years building her company, putting in long hours and planning ahead, plus, she'd already been doing fairly well financially running a successful company. This was no out-of-the-blue lucky strike.

This was the result of hard work, dedication and no small amount of entrepreneurial zeal.

Still, when it was all said and done, she had to be careful about the sudden infusion of massive amounts of cash and not wind up a few years from now, broken, wondering what the hell happened.

The best way to prevent that from happening was to simply take her time.

Starting with right now.

Pauling snapped her laptop closed, slid it into her leather messenger bag and carried it into the bedroom. She had two suitcases on the bed – one big and one small.

Her goal had been to fit everything into the small one, but it hadn't worked. She was now transferring everything to the big one, and adding clothes as she went.

Her mind, for some reason, turned to Jack Reacher.

Talk about polar opposites.

Here she was with more money in the bank than she

knew what to do with, loading a big suitcase. She was living in the same upscale condo she'd had for years, and thinking about acquiring more real estate down the road. Not to mention an investment account that would rival that of a top CEO.

Reacher was somewhere, hiking down the highway, with nothing but freshly bought clothes on his back, an ATM card and a toothbrush. Finding adventure and then, at the end of it all, being the man who just walks away.

Somewhat embarrassed at her sudden reflections on a former lover, she put everything back in the smaller suitcase, and rolled the bigger one back into her closet.

She was going to see Michael Tallon.

It might be better for both of them if she arrived with minimal baggage – in every sense of the word.

Pauling laughed.

Patience, she thought again.

And that applied to more than just money.

"What the hell were you thinking?" Nash barked at Dawkins. The black man was covered in blood. He had gone berserk stabbing the enemy soldier, culminating in a crescendo of slashing, cutting and butchering.

"The man had his chance to cooperate," Dawkins explained, his voice calm, in stark contrast to the blood that covered his dark, heavily muscled torso.

They were back at base camp, a portable trailer with two vehicles and several covered trailers loaded with gear. Inside the main HQ, the men were showering and cleaning their weapons, but Nash was upset.

He'd lost control of his team.

He glanced over at Blatch.

"And you? What's your excuse?"

Nash had seen Blatch drag the woman behind the farm-house and heard her subsequent screams. Blatch had been back there with her for nearly an hour and when he'd returned, alone, he too was covered in blood.

"She had it coming to her," Blatch said softly. He was a

lean mean, built like a greyhound, with red hair and a red beard. His fierce blue eyes flashed from the sea of red like searchlights failing to see anything in the distance.

Nash shook his head. He knew they were going to have to report what had happened on the mission to their superiors, and they wouldn't be happy. He'd be lucky if he still had a job tomorrow. Hell, he'd feel fortunate if he didn't wind up in some maximum security prison somewhere.

He also knew that there was no "we" when it came to making that report. It would be his name, and his alone, on that electronic communication. The leader always bore the brunt of the actions of his men. It's the way it had been and always would be.

Either way, he knew the report would not go over well, which was an enormous understatement.

He set his weapon down and began to break it apart. He'd fired dozens of rounds back at the battle scene, and would have to clean his weapon thoroughly.

"I ought to have both of you court-martialed," Nash said. "I will not allow this to ever happen under my command again."

Dawkins and Blatch stood shoulder to shoulder.

"Look, I'm sorry," Dawkins said. "It's just that I hate cowards. The man didn't even put up a fight and then he was going to run. I'm a soldier. Killing is what I do. Do I wish we could have gotten some information from him first? Of course. All I can do is apologize and vow to be a better soldier, more disciplined."

"Yeah, well that's all well and fine but now we have no idea when and where Zotz will be," Nash said. "If he manages to infiltrate our territory, we'll have failed. Lots of innocent people will die because we messed up."

Blatch shuffled his feet. "I agree with everything

Dawkins said, man. I need to be more professional. I guess when I saw the woman and knew she was one of them, my instincts took over," he explained, ruefully. "It won't happen again."

Nash nodded.

Dawkins and Blatch were the best soldiers he'd ever had under his command. They were elite.

He was just as much to blame as they were for the massacre.

Nash only hoped his superiors would feel the same way.

Tallon had traded in his assault rifle for a broom and a mop.

He really wondered what in the name of God he was doing. He should have just hired someone from town to come and clean his place in preparation of Pauling's arrival.

The problem was, his privacy was important on both a personal and professional level. The little ranch house and compound he'd built for himself had so many parts that were "off-limits" it didn't make sense to hire someone to come in and clean only parts of it. Hell, fifty percent of it would be "off-limits," so what was the point?

Plus, the little town of Independence Springs near the southern borders of Nevada and California was small, and not a lot of luxury services were available.

Which meant he had to do it himself.

And that was fine.

With all of his years spent in the military, he'd gotten pretty self-sufficient and wasn't above cleaning up after himself. The only difference was there's "clean" for a single man, and then there's "clean" for a woman arriving for an extended stay.

So, he cleaned the place from top to bottom, making sure it didn't smell like a "guy."

When that was done, he drove to the supermarket and stocked up on plenty of fresh fruits and vegetables, good wine and gourmet cheeses. He knew Pauling had a taste for some of the slightly finer things than he did, so he wanted to make sure he had some options.

Back home, he stored the purchases and also put some fresh flowers he'd purchased in a vase.

That done, he took a look around and felt fairly confident.

When he'd invited Pauling to perhaps make their relationship more permanent, he wasn't sure how she'd take it. He knew she was fiercely independent and used to being in charge of both her business and her personal life. But they'd worked together several times over the years and the relationship had grown to be something he missed on a daily basis when she wasn't around. Which was why he made the proposition.

He, too, knew he would have to make his own adjustments. He was used to being a bit of a lone wolf and now he would be forced to think of someone other than himself, which was fine because he wasn't a selfish person by nature. And of everyone in the world, Pauling was the person he would want to share it with.

So, he hoped that his home felt warm and welcoming.

Because he didn't just want Pauling to feel at home.

He wanted her to stay.

The businessman's name was Scott Foster. He was from Los Angeles and had made his considerable wealth as a producer on some of Hollywood's biggest films.

In the circles of the rich and famous in Tinseltown his name was very well known.

Which is why on this day he was no longer a businessman.

He was a hunter.

He had purchased the property nearly a decade ago because it fulfilled all of his needs; the hunting lodge was remote, isolated, and none of his associates in California knew anything about it.

It was south of Death Valley near the border with Nevada and getting to the property required an all-wheel drive vehicle as there were no roads.

Power came from a generator and in one of the many outbuildings were several all-terrain vehicles.

Foster had gassed up one of the ATVs and ridden it for

nearly an hour and a half into the barren foothills with nothing but a satellite phone and a high-powered rifle.

He'd been hunting for the better part of the day when he first noticed the buzzards. Since he'd seen nothing up to that point, the sight of the huge birds piqued his curiosity.

Foster wound his way closer to the birds, first on the ATV and then on foot. He was curious what the buzzards were feeding on and if it was a dead animal, what kind. It might also tell him the type of large predators that were active and what they were hunting.

He worked his way closer to the spot below the circling birds but he paused. Just in case whatever might have killed the object of he buzzards' attention was still around.

The building had just come into view and he was a bit surprised. He'd been hunting up here for quite some time and had no idea that a structure even existed here.

Foster stopped several hundred yards away and used high-powered binoculars to get a better look.

What he saw caused him to blink and then blink again.

At first, he wondered if it was a joke. Or maybe he was being filmed, like a practical joke of sorts.

He looked through the binoculars again and watched carefully as the buzzards fought over the lifeless form at the rear of a small farmhouse of sorts. Or maybe it was a deserted hunting cabin and the hunters had carelessly disposed of some entrails.

Foster glanced over at his satellite phone and saw that his signal was plenty strong to make a phone call.

He shook his head, unsure of what he was really seeing.

As a Hollywood producer, he'd brought to the big screen many films that were pure entertainment, often requiring the viewer to suspend disbelief.

Because deep down, everyone knew it was all made up.

Fiction.

So he picked up the binoculars and looked again, willing himself to be wrong.

But he wasn't.

Scott Foster didn't want to believe what he was seeing but his eyes and his mind realized there was only one option.

The buzzards were feeding on the body of a human being.

Pauling settled into her seat in first class on a direct flight out of LaGuardia.

When the flight attendants offered her a beverage, she ordered a gin and tonic.

What the heck, she thought. *I'm unemployed.*

But then she corrected herself because, technically, she was employed by the firm who had bought her out. Part of the deal was an annual consulting fee of $100,000 a year but there were no duties required for it.

As she sipped her drink she thought about what was waiting for her on the other end of this trip.

She and Michael Tallon had a long history.

They had worked together many times and it wasn't until he suggested she leave New York to come and spend time with him that things had gotten serious.

It had simply worked out that as she weighed the offer from Tallon, at the same time, she was contemplating the enormous offer from her biggest and most aggressive competitor. One with very, very deep pockets.

So as much as she considered compromising and saying

yes to one offer and not to the other, she didn't. At this point in her life she knew what she wanted and more importantly, what she didn't want.

So she said yes to both offers.

While selling her firm was permanent, the "yes" to Michael Tallon was more of a test venture. She hadn't made that explicitly clear to Tallon, but Pauling was fairly certain he knew. He wasn't exactly the new kid on the block, and neither was she.

Pauling looked at some of the other passengers in first class, most of them men. They were hunched over their respective laptops working furiously, combing through spreadsheets and PowerPoint presentations, probably ready to hit the ground running as soon as they landed.

She closed her eyes and thought about her past relationships, some of them serious and some not so serious.

Again, she thought of Reacher and how that was one of the few relationships where it wasn't serious, but she had wanted it to be. Most times, it was the other way around.

But that wasn't Reacher's way, she understood that. And had made peace with the knowledge.

Pauling looked out her window and saw a mountain range pass underneath them, making her feel like she was crossing borders and entering new territory.

She was happy. No doubt about it. She was very much looking forward to seeing Tallon, spending time with him and that feeling was without reservation. It was liberating and for the first time in a long time, she felt pure freedom.

Pauling cared very deeply about Tallon and when the wheels of the plane touched down she moved quickly through the terminal, retrieved her bag and spotted a person holding a sign.

The letters on the sign had caught her eye. They were big, block letters spelling out PAULING.

And beneath the sign was a handsome and extremely well-built man.

Pauling smiled.

Michael Tallon.

Sheriff Melanie Bordeau parked her cruiser in the driveway of the remote farmhouse and shut off the engine.

It had already been a long morning and now she was having to deal with what she was sure would turn out to be a hoax or a misunderstanding. Or, as often was the case, a hunter suffering from a monumental hangover so severe it created hallucinations.

Over the years, she'd gotten calls from hunters who'd seen Bigfoot, werewolves and ghosts. In one instance, all at the same time.

Eventually, they'd all admitted they were either horribly hungover or detoxing from drugs. In one case – it was an absence of drugs. A hunter from San Diego had forgotten his prescription antidepressants and withdrawal had caused him to see his dead grandmother throwing her famous homemade biscuits at him.

Bordeau glanced up in the sky and noted the buzzards.

Well, that might be something, she thought.

The call from dispatch had said a hunter had found a

dead body. A human body, which was why she had been skeptical. This was hunting country, as well as home to plenty of bears and mountain lions. Deer carcasses had a way of showing up repeatedly and once in awhile some person with a good imagination assumed the body was human.

Bordeau had a feeling this was going to be another simple misunderstanding and she could get back to her regular routine of checking hunting licenses and settling innocuous domestic disputes.

She left the cruiser and approached a man who was sitting astride an ATV. Bordeau could see the hunting rifle in its scabbard strapped to the side of the vehicle.

The man slid off the ATV and approached her.

"Hello officer," he said.

He was a tall man, with perfect hair and white teeth. She immediately assumed he was a wealthy businessman from Los Angeles, out "roughing" it in his Ralph Lauren hunting clothes.

"Afternoon," she replied. "You called in about a body?"

"Yeah, it's behind the house," he said.

"What's your name?" Bordeau asked.

"Scott Foster."

"You live around here?"

"No, I live in Los Angeles. I have a place about twenty miles to the west. A hunting cabin. That's what I was doing when I saw the buzzards, so I drove over."

Melanie nodded.

"Okay, stay here while I take a look." She pointed him toward her cruiser, away from his rifle, which was still on his ATV, and walked toward the rear of the structure.

She kept Foster in view, as well as the vehicle.

It was a clear day, full sun, and hot. The air was dry and

the brown grass crunched beneath her shoes. The house wasn't much, a single-story cabin with unpainted, weathered wood and dirty windows.

Bordeau reached the rear of the house and took a wide, cautious turn, her hand on the butt of her pistol.

One look told her Foster had been right. It most certainly was a human body, even after the buzzards had finished tearing it apart. She walked closer and studied the remains, the smell reaching her nostrils and nearly triggering a gag reflex. Bordeau noticed the long hair and the small cowboy boots.

A woman.

She backed away until she could see Foster standing near her cruiser.

"Did you go inside?" she asked him.

"No, I thought I'd better not," he said.

"Okay, stay there."

Bordeau retraced her steps until she reached the house's back door. She'd noticed that it was slightly ajar. She withdrew her gun and held it in front of her.

"Anyone home?" she called out.

There was no answer.

She used her foot to push the door all the way open and took a quick peek around the doorjamb.

"Holy shit," she said, ducking back from the open door.

What she'd seen had shocked her. A large, empty room, with multiple dead bodies on the floor. Dried blood everywhere.

Bordeau keyed the radio on her shoulder and asked for backup.

She raised her gun, held it in front of her, took a deep breath, and stepped into the room.

8

Blatch wasn't satisfied.

Oh sure, he'd had a little bit of fun with the woman but he'd been a little too eager and he actually killed her when he still really wasn't quite satisfied.

He hated that. It was like going to a movie and then the projector breaks down and you never get to see the end of the film.

His fantasies were very elaborately created down to the most minute of detail and when the video didn't match the one in his head, it created a jarring effect that ruined the whole thing.

It simply wouldn't do.

He knew that Nash was really pissed off at him and Dawkins, too. They'd both screwed up once again. One of these days he was worried that Nash would kick him off the team. And he didn't want that. He loved fighting alongside this crew.

Nash was one of the good guys. If there was only one fault Nash possessed it was that he didn't have the best control of his men. Blatch felt guilty even thinking about it.

Especially now because he knew what he was going to do.

It was close to midnight and Nash and Dawkins had already turned in for the night. In their minds, the mission was done. But he, Blatch, wasn't even close to being finished.

No, he was going to go out there and finish the thing so it matched the movie in his head. Only then could he sleep.

He slipped out of his room, let himself out of the command trailer and drove down to the little redneck bar on the outskirts of town. No one there knew him and Nash had said the bar was strictly off-limits while they were doing their operation.

Blatch took a seat at the bar and ordered a beer.

The bartender was a woman and a little more masculine than Blatch usually liked. She had thick, broad shoulders and there was a weird tattoo on her upper back.

She smiled at him when he ordered a beer. There were only a few other people in the bar and two of them looked like high schoolers wearing guilty expressions as if they'd sneaked in with a fake ID.

There were also a couple of guys who'd probably been drinking since their softball game finished...and they lost.

Blatch would wait them out because the upside of the bartender being a bit masculine was that she represented a challenge.

Blatch liked it when they not only fought, but they fought well. It made his victory that much more gratifying.

He slowly drank his beer and had no intention of getting drunk. The bartender was sneaking little glances at him and he knew from experience she was interested.

Blatch looked at his lean, long face in the mirror and liked how his bright red hair contrasted with his blue eyes.

He smiled back at the bartender so she would know that she was definitely going to get what she wanted.

And a whole lot more.

9

"That's it?" Tallon asked Pauling, a smile on his face, after they'd kissed and embraced. He was pointing at her luggage, or, more accurately, the lack of it.

Pauling understood the point. She'd only brought one bag, implying this wasn't a permanent move.

"Packing light – it's an old habit," she said.

He laughed, but she still felt a twinge of guilt. After all, Tallon had been the one who'd pushed for her to come out and spend time with him on a more regular basis. When she'd agreed, he may have been expecting a more long-term commitment.

She didn't blame him for perhaps being a bit surprised at just how much of a test run this trip was.

But ever since she'd agreed to sell her company, Pauling had been telling herself to take things slowly. The worst approach would be to make a bunch of important life decisions in a short amount of time. No longer being in charge of her own company was a huge adjustment.

No sense in making another.

"If you're planning on supplementing with shopping, don't get your hopes up," he told her.

The little town of Independence Springs was nestled in the southwestern crook of Death Valley. Pauling knew it was a modest little city with a quiet main street, a few big box retailers at the edge of town and lots of wide-open spaces.

"No one shops in stores anymore," she said. "It's all online."

Tallon maneuvered his 4x4 onto the freeway.

"Congratulations again on the sale. How do you feel?" Tallon asked.

"I would imagine it feels a little like sending your kid off to college. I raised my company from scratch, and built it into something I was really proud of. But I passed on some opportunities to make it even larger than it was, because I'd set a certain standard," Pauling said. "Now, I feel like my company's all grown up and I can only watch it from a distance."

"You can still visit, right?" Tallon said.

Pauling laughed. "Yeah, but I'm not sure I want to. Technically, I'm a consultant, but I think some breathing room is in order. Both for myself and the new owners."

Tallon nodded.

The freeway wound through some red and dusty foothills before descending into some desert flats. The land was so vast and empty, Pauling almost felt a sense of vertigo. She was so used to the claustrophobic nature of New York City. Coming out here was like being on a long flight to some exotic destination. The change in scenery could almost be a shock.

It wasn't long before they pulled up in front of Tallon's house. Pauling loved the adobe ranch, and marveled at how well he had incorporated his need for home defense without ruining the architectural integrity of the place.

As Tallon pulled into the driveway she drank in the view with the mountains in the distance, the setting sun and the beauty of Tallon's home. It was like a western landscape painting and she couldn't wait to explore the hills beyond the home.

"Lovely, as always," she said. She'd only been to the ranch once, but it was even prettier than she'd remembered.

Tallon was all business unloading her suitcase and showing her into the home. She could smell something delicious in the oven.

"Some baked quail – I finally figured out how to set the timer on the stove."

Pauling laughed.

"I hope it won't be done for awhile," she said as she slid into his arms.

I t was the most secretive building on base.

Located adjacent to the command center's head-quarters, it was a single-story structure with rein-forced concrete walls and, many surmised, an underground bunker. On its roof were several sets of elaborate antennas and satellite dishes most presumed were built to enable secure and classified transmission of information.

They were partly right.

They were also partly wrong in the sense that the tech-nology wasn't designed to transmit, rather, it was built to defend. As in, prevent eavesdropping and/or any leakage of classified information.

It was here, in the base near Death Valley, that the U.S. Army had designed and built a massive compound for the "new" war on terrorism. Any innovations in the battle against extremists almost always emerged from this highly isolated and hidden-from-public base.

Now, in the secret building a small group of men convened in the structure's only conference room. It, too, benefited from the latest technology designed to ensure all conversations were kept private. For eternity. No records, either on paper or digitally produced, were allowed. Once the last echoes of spoken words dissipated, they would be gone forever.

There were two men in the room, polar opposites of each other. The older of the two was Crawford – a solid brick of a man with close-cropped silver hair, a deeply lined, tanned face, and piercing blue eyes.

Across from him was a man ten years his junior, if not more. He had unkempt hair, a scraggly beard and wire-rimmed glasses. He wore a dark suit and tie.

They sat in silence until a third man entered.

He wore standard issue Army BDUs and assumed a deferential posture toward Crawford. His name tag said Lucas.

"What the hell is going on?" Crawford barked at him, before he had a chance to even sit down.

"I'm afraid Dr. Aldrich and I haven't had a chance to discuss the situation," Lucas replied, nodding his head toward the unkempt man in the dark suit.

"Well, discuss it now then for Chrissakes!" Crawford said, his tone filled with exasperation.

"There is no reason for alarm," Dr. Aldrich said. He had a subdued voice, almost clinical and robotic. Probably to hypnotize his patients, Crawford thought.

"We had a minor breach in security, I know that," Lucas said. "But that loophole, if you will, is now closed. We are in the process of reclaiming any assets that were unwittingly dispersed."

Crawford rolled his eyes.

"How did it happen?" he asked Lucas.

"We perhaps underestimated the skills of the men involved. They were able to take out two guards, breech the security perimeter, and escape into darkness," Lucas explained while Dr. Aldrich sat, looking bored with the discussion. "By the time we learned they'd absconded, it was too late. But we're zeroing in, in terms of location. This will be resolved quickly and quietly."

"It better be," Crawford said.

Aldrich laughed quietly and even rolled his eyes.

Crawford slammed his fist down on the table. "I'm going to see to it that you are shut down," he said to the doctor.

"Not possible," Aldrich replied, his voice still calm and mechanical. "That can only be done by those above you in pay grade. You are powerless. Impotent, even."

Lucas recoiled visibly as he watched Crawford's tanned face turn crimson.

"Listen, you mealy mouthed piece of shit," Crawford growled. "If you don't get your act together, I'll see to it you never work for the military again. Hell, maybe you'll never work for anyone, ever."

"Is that a threat, General?" Dr. Aldrich answered, his voice icy.

Crawford ignored him and turned to Lucas.

"Get this cleaned up, or you'll be tossed onto the trash heap along with this batshit loser."

He stood and stalked from the room.

After a long pause, Aldrich sighed and turned to Lucas.

"Why did you lie?"

11

T he room smelled of blood and death. A metallic, almost coppery odor, combined with the basest scents the human body can produce.

Especially in death, when the body releases everything it has.

There was no doubt in Sheriff Melanie Bordeau's mind that she was about to embark on a case unlike any other she'd ever experienced.

Of course, she thought of her critics, when it came to said experience.

Or lack thereof, according to them.

She was young, her 30th birthday was still three months away, and many claimed she only got the job because her father, Henry Bordeau, had been sheriff for the past three decades.

As she surveyed the carnage in the room, though, all thoughts of her critics disappeared, blotted about by the sight of horrific, violent death.

This had clearly been no ordinary shooting. This had none of the hallmarks of a drunken disagreement among hunters gone wrong. Or a neighborly squabble turned deadly.

No, this was something else.

The room was relatively bare, with some rustic furniture that had clearly seen better days. An open kitchen was off to the right, with a tiny stove and a makeshift countertop. Two wooden stools sat near the counter. To the left of the furniture was a pile of blankets and some firewood that looked like it had been hastily gathered.

Transients? Bordeau wondered.

Careful not to touch anything and disturb evidence, Bordeau stepped closer to the first victim, a dark-skinned man. His hands were tied behind his back. He'd clearly been savagely beaten, his throat slit, multiple stab wounds and maybe even tortured. Although she doubted he'd lived long enough to endure much, judging by the size of the slash across his throat.

Behind him, on the floor, were two more bodies. They were both males, but younger. It was hard to tell as they were covered in blood and both of them had been shot in the head. They too had been bound.

Bordeau noticed a blanket between the two sets of bodies. She poked it with the tip of her finger.

It was wet.

She walked around the bodies, studied the worn wooden floor and spotted several shell casings. They were a size she wasn't familiar with but they didn't look like typical hunting cartridges.

Also, she noticed there was no real sign of struggle. The woman who had been killed behind the house must have gone there under her own power, or possibly dragged. But she had definitely been killed outside.

Outside, she heard the sound of a vehicle approaching and slowly backed from the room.

At the front of the building, another officer had arrived, along with a van carrying the county coroner. He would process the scene, and gather any forensic evidence.

Bordeau's mind was already working through the logistics of what may have happened here.

She knew this was no conventional homicide.

No, something else was involved.

Either drugs.

The military.

Or both.

12

Nash felt like a house that had barely survived hurricane-force winds.

He'd just gotten off the phone with his commanding officer who had threatened him with everything from physical harm to sexual assault to eviction from the army.

The message had been abundantly clear: get your troops in order or you'll be the one on the firing line.

Now, he stood watching as Dawkins and Blatch finished preparing for their next operation.

The command trailer was starting to smell like a locker room that hadn't seen a janitor in weeks. They'd had a large pot of coffee and the air was a mixture of fresh coffee grounds, gun oil, and male sweat.

Nash wondered how much longer they would be stationed out here. Until the job was done, probably.

And then what?

He wondered, but in his line of work it didn't pay to look too far ahead.

Instead, he studied his men.

Dawkins seemed fine, but Nash couldn't stop looking at Blatch. Something about the red-haired man seemed off.

"You okay, Blatch?" he asked him.

Blatch glanced up, a bit too quickly, his blue eyes slightly wider than normal *Was he anxious, or desperately trying to appear innocent*, Nash wondered.

"Yeah, why?"

Nash stared him down until Blatch went back to assembling his gear.

Dawkins finished first.

"Ready," he said.

They both waited for Blatch to finish and then Nash brought them over to the operations table where a map had been pinned to the top.

Nash tapped a valley no more than five miles away.

"I was just briefed and the latest intel has Zotz possibly arriving here," he said. "We're not sure the exact time, but word is it should happen within the next twenty-four hours."

"If this guy's so dangerous, how is he able to move around like this?" Dawkins asked. "It's crazy."

Nash didn't have an answer ready. "That's for the big chiefs to know, not us little Indians," he said. "All I know is we need to be there and nail this nutjob to the wall."

"So Zotz is a terrorist? Here to recruit others? Or meet with a cell he's already established?"

"That wasn't in the briefing," Nash said. "Above our pay grade. But it's safe to say that whatever he's got planned, it's big and will involve a lot of innocent people being killed. Unless we kill him first."

"Let's do this," Blatch said.

They mustered out into the vehicle but Nash was still wondering what was wrong with Blatch.

He seemed distracted.

In their line of work, distraction was deadly.

13

Sheriff Bordeau studied the forensic report.

The shell casings appeared to be 9 x 19mm Parabellum – a standard military cartridge.

The footprints at the rear of the house also appeared to be from a military-type boot.

They had yet to find any form of ID on the dead bodies and the more detailed analysis of any fibers would take at least a few days. There was a backup at the crime lab, as always, and even though it was the first multiple homicide in the area in years, Bordeau didn't think her case would be expedited.

The door to her office opened and a shadow fell across the room.

She glanced up and saw her father standing in the doorway.

"Hey," he said.

Henry Bordeau was a legend in the county, and physically he lived up to the myth. It seemed he was almost as broad as he was tall. He was like a buffalo wearing a cowboy hat.

Even though he was over seventy years old, he still had an air of solidity, giving off the impression that he would be here long after you, no matter the age difference. His face was craggy, partially hidden behind a thick beard and a bulbous nose whose spider veins were probably half-full of his favorite scotch.

The big man dropped his bulk into the chair across from his daughter's desk. He looked around the office and she imagined he was envisioning the way he used to have it, with his mounted fish and hunting trophies.

"Heard you caught a quadruple," he growled at her.

"Sure did," she said. "A bad one. Torture. And we think one of the vics, a woman, was raped, too. That's classified, though, so don't tell anyone."

Her father shook his massive head.

"Sick bastards," he said. "Do you think it was hunters?"

The transient population of hunters who came and went in the area during various hunting seasons often had a bad reputation among the locals. They were known to ignore game laws, get drunk in town, and in general treat the place like it was one giant hotel room they could trash on their way out.

"Don't think so," she said. "But we don't have much yet in way of evidence. Just a hunch."

"You need any help?" he asked.

Melanie Bordeau was tempted to roll her eyes but she kept her face straight. She knew the old man just wanted to help, but she'd been very clear about not wanting him to overstep his bounds ever since she was elected sheriff.

"Not yet, but we'll see what happens."

He nodded, obviously disappointed but keeping it to himself. He heaved himself out of the chair and went to the door.

"Be careful," he said. "It sounds like maybe more than just a one-off. Especially if they didn't get what they were looking for."

She watched her father walk out of the office and voices greeting him on his way out.

Melanie thought about what he'd said.

Maybe they didn't get what they were looking for.

How did he know she suspected there was more than one killer?

14

A fter her father left the office, Bordeau thought about what she'd learned from the initial report.

This part of the country was definitely pro-gun. Not just because of the hunters. But also, homeowners. Home defense was a serious issue and westerners preferred to take matters into their own hands, literally. Nearly every home out here had a rifle or shotgun hanging over the fireplace, or a big revolver under the bed.

Guns were everywhere in the West.

Plus, there was no shortage of ex-military in the area with all of the army bases scattered around. This region was perfect for the government to build installations in the middle of nowhere. Wide, vast deserts nearly entirely devoid of population were often the choice of military planners who wanted to be able to develop certain things in private.

Bordeau, or more accurately, her father, had known plenty of ex-military people now living in the region.

But in the back of her mind Bordeaux seemed to remember something. An incident at a local bar involving a mysterious loner who may have been ex-military, maybe even special ops.

Bordeau racked her brain trying to remember the incident.

She went onto her computer and accessed the incident files from the past year or so, entering keywords like special ops, military, lone man, etc.

Nothing came back.

Where had she heard the story about the bar?

It had to have been at Rooster's, the main bar in town. Bordeau's friend Connie ran the place, maybe that was where she'd heard the tale.

Bordeau got up from her desk and headed for her squad car.

She would drop in at Rooster's and see what she could find out.

15

Bordeau drove into downtown Independence Springs, and went several blocks south, past a laundromat and a Chinese restaurant until she came to the parking lot for Rooster's.

The bar was a low-slung building probably erected in the seventies, with a fake Spanish tile roof and a six-foot rooster perched over the entrance. Every year around high school graduation some kids would always get the idea to try to steal the rooster. That is, until they met the razor wire surrounding it, as well as the motion lights.

Not to mention, the squad cars that regularly patrolled the area on graduation night.

Bordeau parked her squad car and went into Rooster's. It had a long bar on one side, some pool tables, a jukebox and a half-dozen tables and chairs. On the walls were reprints of old western paintings, shootouts with cowboys, mostly Remingtons or Russells. Bordeau could never keep those two artists straight.

Her friend was tending bar.

"Hey Connie."

Connie Higgins was a lean, athletic woman with blonde hair and a chiseled face. Bordeau had known her for several years and the two had become friends, bonding over being in charge of their respective businesses. The sheriff knew her friend was divorced, a brief marriage to a college sweetheart, and the two often talked about the lack of qualified candidates in the romance department of little Independence Springs.

After they exchanged some pleasantries Bordeaux said, "Hey, do you remember telling me a story about a guy hassling you and then another guy kicked his ass in the parking lot?"

Connie put a glass of sparkling water with a lime in front of Bordeau. She cocked her head to one side and squinted her hazel eyes as she tried to remember.

"Yeah, actually I do remember," she said with a smile. "I didn't see it happen, but the rumor is the guy put an awful big hurt on Ronnie Kudlow. Remember him? Caveman kind of guy always loose with his hands?"

Bordeau did remember him.

"It was great, because Ronnie never set foot in here again. Heard he moved up to Denver, thank God."

"And you thought that guy was some kind of special ops?"

"Yeah, I remember that."

"Did he tell you his name?"

"Yeah, I remember that because he said it was Tallon, and I said, you mean like the claw?" Connie said, holding up her fingers and hooking them. "And he laughed and said it was with two Ls. As in Tallon."

"Interesting," Bordeau said.

"Yeah, the funny thing is, I never saw him again, either. I could've sworn he said he lived in the area but I had never seen him before and he hasn't been in since. Which is a shame because he was a looker," Connie said, shooting Bordeau a lascivious wink.

Bordeau laughed, they made small talk and when she finished her sparkling water, she left.

Back in the office, Bordeau logged onto a database of citizens taxpayer records and found the name Michael Tallon. She saw his address and knew it was on the outskirts of town. It could possibly be that little adobe ranch she'd always admired from a distance.

Bordeau thought about it and it sounded to her like this Tallon was maybe some kind of vigilante. Not afraid to take the law into his own hands.

And if he had a special ops background maybe he might know of other military people in the area.

Bordeau closed her browser window, got to her feet and went out to her squad car.

She would pay Michael Tallon a visit first thing in the morning.

16

"There's no way Zotz is in there," Dawkins said.

They were on a narrow, two-lane highway barely one step up from a dirt road. It wound its way north and south, skirting major valleys, but dipping in and out of draws and taking huge, sweeping curves. When the road had been made, it had clearly been constructed on a small budget because every obstacle was avoided, rather than eliminated.

"Probably not, but information may be," Nash answered. "Hope for the best, plan for the worst."

Blatch was driving and they were a half-mile behind their target: a nondescript motor home with several large antennas on its roof.

They were in a black passenger van with four-wheel drive and oversized tires. They were ready for battle, on edge.

"Up there, you know what to do," Nash said, pointing ahead to a spot in the distance.

The road topped out on a ridge and then descended into a long, narrow valley. Once the van was at the crest, they could see all the way down the valley, at least three miles and the road was clear.

Blatch gunned the van and they pulled up alongside the motorhome. Dirt and dust were spewing from beneath the motorhome's huge tires making visibility difficult. Smaller stones and pebbles bounced off the side of the van, sounding to Nash a little too similar to small arms fire.

"Go!" he shouted.

Behind him, Dawkins slid open the side passenger door of the van as Blatch pulled the vehicle so close Nash could reach out and touch the motorhome's rear taillight.

Dawkins timed his jump and leapt from the van onto the rear ladder of the motorhome, his assault rifle strapped to his back.

"He's clear!" Nash shouted, allowing Blatch to veer away from the bigger vehicle.

Dawkins climbed the ladder and crawled along the top of the motorhome, as Blatch gunned the van forward. Once they were past the bigger vehicle, Blatch cut across in front, forcing it to slow.

The horn sounded from the motorhome, angry and impatient.

Both vehicles skidded to a stop in a cloud of dust, dirt and stone.

Nash leapt from the van and ran to the side door of the motorhome, his rifle raised. Peering inside, he saw no one so he opened fire, shattering the door until it came off its hinge.

Blatch raced around the other side of the van, hurrying to the rear of the vehicle to cut off anyone trying to escape.

Nash climbed the stairs into the motorhome, turned, and saw Dawkins drop into the rear of the vehicle through the skylight.

Inside the vehicle, it was silent except for someone crying.

"Please, what do you want?" a man asked. He was a skinny white man in a button-down shirt. Next to him, a young woman stared at him, not as scared as the man, but terrified nonetheless.

There stared at Nash.

"Where's Zotz?" he asked.

The two people, a man and a woman, looked at Nash.

"Who? Why did you do this?"

Dawkins stepped up behind them. The man looked at the big black man, saw the enormous knife.

"We called 9-1-1," he said. "You can't hurt us."

Dawkins laughed. Nash looked at the woman and knew Blatch would be eager to start his handiwork on her.

"I'm going to give you one last chance," Nash said. "Tell us where Zotz is, or when he will be here, and you'll live."

"We don't know anyone named Zotz, you asshole!" the woman screamed at him, her voice hysterical.

Nash sighed and shot both of them in the head.

17

P auling awoke disoriented.

For a moment she thought she was back in New York in her condo. But soon, the utter silence, completely devoid of traffic sounds and cars honking, made her realize she was somewhere else. And when the sounds of Tallon's gentle breathing reached her ears she remembered where she was.

They'd had a wonderful reunion, most of it spent in bed, except for occasional breaks for nutritional reinforcement.

She'd told Tallon about the final process of selling her company, and he'd filled her in on what his last few projects had been, although much of what he told her was somewhat vague. She didn't take it personally, knowing that much of it was classified and that he was withholding information for her own good. The less she knew certain details, the better.

Pauling pulled the sheets back carefully, slid from the bed and padded into the kitchen where the coffee was ready. Tallon's coffee machine had a timer, designed to start brewing fairly early. Maybe it was the aroma of freshly made coffee that had awoken her.

She stood at the counter, saw the first shafts of morning light bring the distance foothills to life. Pauling was looking forward to doing some exploring, getting to know the land her significant other – she could call him that now – had chosen for his home base.

The doorbell rang and Pauling knew it wasn't the coffee that had roused her from sleep. A car must have pulled into the driveway.

Behind her, Tallon emerged from the bedroom and went straight into his office where she knew he had his home security monitors.

"You've got to be kidding me," he said, emerging from his office, his hair tousled, eyeing the cup of coffee jealously in Pauling's hands.

"What is it?" she asked.

He sighed.

"Cops."

18

"I didn't lie," Lucas responded to Dr. Aldrich.

They were still sitting in the conference room. Crawford had stormed out, but his lingering presence and his hostility were still being felt.

"Withholding the truth is presenting a false narrative," Aldrich said. He was stroking his scraggly beard and Lucas knew why Crawford hated the man so much. Not only was he a snobby intellectual and about as far from a fighting man as you could get, the doctor was slovenly with his unkempt hair and flakes of dandruff on his black suit coat.

Lucas had done his research on the man and knew that while brilliant, he was also prone to slightly criminal behavior ranging from petty theft to sexual assault. It was why the scrawny intellectual had been booted from prestigious universities and fell into the lap of the military.

The truth was, he'd had very few options.

"For which you should be thanking me," Lucas said.

"You did that to help yourself," Dr. Aldrich replied. "Don't tell me it was for me because he has no control over my work."

It's not your work I would be worried about, Lucas thought, but he kept the notion to himself. He needed the doctor to focus.

"So what are you going to do now?" the doctor asked. His tone clearly conveyed he wasn't very interested even though Lucas knew he ought to be.

"Establish containment and hopefully retrieval as soon as possible."

"Nash will seek to establish something similar to his last deployment," Dr. Aldrich said. "A command base. Headquarters, whatever you people call it. He'll be focused on his objective and working with Dawkins and Blatch. He must be found as soon as possible so I can get him back under observation. It's imperative or he may do something that will go beyond anything we had planned. It would be a disaster."

Aldrich said it with a flat monotone that suggested he didn't care one way or the other.

"I've got aerial surveillance, as well as more boots on the ground. If he's out there, we'll find him. Part of it depends on how well he conceals himself."

"He's a soldier," Dr. Aldrich said. "Highly accomplished. It won't be easy."

They sat in silence for a moment.

"I have to ask. Does it matter–" Lucas struggled to find the right way to phrase it.

"Of course it matters," Aldrich interjected, cutting him off. "You have to bring him back alive."

19

The door opened and Sheriff Bordeau was facing a tall man with broad shoulders and eyes that were curious, not defiant or nervous.

"Michael Tallon?" she asked.

He nodded. "Sheriff, how can I help you?"

Bordeau noted that he had already studied who she was, probably via a security system somewhere. Military guys loved hardware and she figured Tallon was no exception. That, and the adobe casita had the feeling of a fortress. Albeit, a stylish fortress.

From behind him, she saw a woman, strikingly beautiful, gazing at her. The woman had blonde-ish hair with highlights. A little older than Bordeau would have thought, but the green eyes were striking.

"Hello," the woman said, with a raspy voice that could've belonged to a whiskey and cigarette jazz singer from the 1920s.

"Good morning," Bordeau replied. "I was wondering if you wouldn't mind answering a few questions."

"Not at all," Tallon easily answered. "Want a cup of

coffee?" He was relaxed and casual as he stepped aside and Bordeau entered the room.

"This is Lauren Pauling," he said, gesturing to the woman.

"I'm Sheriff Bordeau," she said as the woman regarded her with a frank appraisal, the green eyes curious.

Bordeau took in the room. It was spacious, well decorated and the furniture was clearly well-made and expensive, but not showy. The floor was a dark wood, the area rug colorful and possibly Native American.

Tallon returned with a cup of coffee and they gathered in the living room. Tallon slid into a leather couch and Pauling hovered near the kitchen. Not a part of the conversation, but certainly within earshot.

Bordeau took a leather club chair across from Tallon.

"Beautiful place you have here," she said. "I always wondered what the inside looked like."

"Thank you," he replied, gazing at her with that same curious expression.

Finally, she plowed ahead.

"Did you hear about the incident out at Tucker's Glade?" Bordeau asked. It was the general location of the killing but was broad enough to encompass a very large area.

"Nope," Tallon replied. "Where is that?"

She studied his expression. Eyes clear, his face untroubled. If he was lying, he was very good at it.

"It's about a dozen miles out of town. Kind of in the middle of nowhere."

"No, never heard of it, actually," he said. "What kind of incident?"

"It happened around noon or so yesterday. Any idea where you were?"

"I was at McCarran picking her up," Tallon said, referring to the airport outside Las Vegas, which was the closest airport to Death Valley.

"Any witnesses?"

He pondered the question. "Well, I went into baggage claim with a big sign that had her name on it," he said, smiling a little bit. "I know some people on her flight saw me. Plus, you can certainly track my cell phone as we were texting back and forth about her arrival."

Bordeau nodded. She believed him, for now. And he was right, she would be able to track his cell phone, although that wasn't necessarily proof of where he was, just his phone. The eyewitnesses at the airport would be a different matter. She would have to contact the airline, get the names and contact information for the other passengers and call them. It would take a lot of legwork, but it could be done.

"What happened at noon or so yesterday?" Tallon asked.

"We had a multiple homicide," she said, carefully watching his expression. It didn't change.

"Why are you here asking me about it?" Tallon wondered. His tone wasn't threatening or confrontational, just interested in her answer.

"There may or may not be a military connection to the killings. I heard you were Special Ops and maybe you could help. Any other ex-military in the area you know about?"

"No, ma'am," Tallon said. "I chose this place for its solitude and I haven't met anyone out here. Then again, my work takes me away a lot of time."

"What is it you do?"

"Private security, mostly."

Bordeau took a sip of coffee while she pondered her next question.

"How long have you lived here?" she asked, glancing around the room.

"About five years or so."

"Like it?"

"I do," he said. "It's home."

Bordeau set down her coffee cup and pulled out one of her business cards. "I won't keep you any longer," she said. "But if you do think of anything, or hear anything that might help me in the case, I would appreciate a call. My cell phone is on there, too."

"Ok, will do," Tallon said.

Bordeau got up, nodded to Pauling who was in the kitchen, watching her with an expression that was hard to read.

"Nice to meet you," Bordeau said to her.

"You too."

Tallon opened the door for her and Bordeau walked out, climbed into her squad car and drove away.

She believed Tallon when he said he didn't know anything about the murders.

So why was she so intrigued by him?

20

She had two first names and was relentlessly teased about it. Katy Sally was a fitness enthusiast with a fairly large Instagram following, currently training for a triathlon in California.

Always a strong swimmer and cyclist, she was focusing on her running, which explained why she was alone in the canyons just south of Death Valley, pounding along a deserted highway with the sun beating down on her.

When she'd crested the hill the motorhome parked along the side of the road caught her attention. Being a woman, alone, in the middle of nowhere was always problematic. However, she had a canister of pepper spray, as well as a tiny pocket knife held snugly in a small pocket inside her running shorts.

Without breaking stride, Katy Sally found the pepper spray canister and unsnapped it from the belt at her waist so it was in her hand. She rotated it to put the trigger under her finger, just in case a kidnapper jumped from the rear of the motorhome and tried to drag her inside.

It was a crazy idea, but there were plenty of true stories that were even worse.

Running downhill, she picked up speed and passed the motorhome, keeping it in view out of the corner of her eye.

Which is how she saw the body sprawled facedown on the far side of the motorhome, near the front bumper.

A trick, she thought.

Katy bore down and ran even faster, but in her mind's eye she saw the pool of blood around the body and slowed.

Finally, she stopped and looked back.

She saw the first body.

And behind it, a second.

No matter how much her instincts told her to keep running, she ignored them and slowly walked back toward the motorhome.

She stopped twenty feet from the sight of the carnage, and unsnapped the case holding her phone firmly against her midsection. She powered the phone on and saw she had two bars of signal strength.

Enough to call 9-1-1.

21

Nash was furious.

"Are you insane?" he shouted at Blatch. They were back in the command center, Blatch's shirt covered in blood, a stupid, leering expression on his face. Things had not gone well on their latest attempt to find Zotz. Another dead end, in every sense of the phrase.

"The woman was a threat!" Blatch shouted.

"I shot her in the head," Nash answered. "Exactly how was she a threat?"

"She refused to follow orders."

"I know the feeling."

"Plus, I didn't think she was dead. It looked like she was sort of edging back toward that closet at the back of the motorhome. Who knew what was in there?"

"There was nothing in there and she wasn't edging anywhere. She was dead, with half her brains splattered onto the big screen television."

"Did you see the size of that thing?" Dawkins asked. "That was a sweet ride."

Both Blatch and Nash ignored him.

"Yeah, we know there was nothing in that closet now," Blatch said, continuing to argue. "But at the time there could have been guns or even more bad guys hiding in there. I had to make sure."

"But you had to molest her dead body? You locked yourself and her in the bedroom of the motorhome and did whatever it is you do with her – that's how you disarm a threat? Not to mention, possibly leave evidence at a crime scene. What were you thinking?"

"I think I was pretty thorough," Blatch laughed.

Behind him, Nash heard Dawkins laugh, too.

At that point, he lost it.

He lunged at Blatch and drove his fist straight into Blatch's face. He felt the cartilage squash under the blow and blood splattered into the air.

Blatch sagged on his feet and Nash drove a knee into his midsection, then threw a wicked uppercut that caught the underside of Blatch's chin and snapped his teeth together with such force that a chip flew off and hit Nash in the eye.

"No!" Dawkins shouted.

But it was too late.

Nash had grabbed a flashlight nearly a foot long and crashed it down on the back of Blatch's head. The sound was sickening: like an axe hitting a rotted tree stump.

Blatch crashed to the floor and Nash pounded the flashlight into the fallen man's head repeatedly until blood coated his hand. He rolled Blatch over and saw the man's lifeless eyes staring aback at him.

"Jesus, you killed him," Dawkins said, peering over Nash's shoulder.

"Yeah. Should've done it a long time ago."

22

Lucas never had difficulty reconciling what he did for a living with his own moral code. His mission was a higher calling, the safety of his country, family and friends.

Sometimes, the lines became a little blurred in how much the end justified the means. Most of the time, he could easily rationalize what he was doing.

Except, that is, when he had to deal with Larkin.

Rarely was the veil lifted for the public to get glimpses of just how seedy and amoral rogue agents among the military forces could become. Usually, they were identified and discharged with all due haste.

Occasionally, a news story would appear and a few service members might be charged with petty crimes, or rarer still, something severe like murder.

The public would move on, satisfied that the extremely rare "bad actors" were caught, punished and relieved of command.

Occasionally, however, these men were never caught, but instead, knowledge of their utter disregard for both army protocol and other people's lives never saw the light of day. Instead, they became well-known to the military underground and ultimately, channeled into unofficial projects.

Such was the case with Larkin.

His background was highly classified, however, Lucas knew it was replete with off-the-books assassinations. No job was too dirty, and while other mercenaries often stated an aversion to killing women and children, Larkin declared nothing off-limits. If enough money was involved, Larkin would end anyone's life, anywhere, any time.

Even worse, the rumor was Larkin also put no restrictions on the people for whom he would work. Drug dealers. Pimps. Organized crime. None of it mattered one iota to Larkin.

Those were rumors, though, and Lucas had no way to confirm if any of it was true. What he did know was that every time he shared space with the man, he felt an inner dread, as if he was venturing into a dark and dangerous place, alone.

All Lucas knew was that when he sat down with the man in the same secret building on the base near Death Valley, he felt a dark cloud pass over his soul.

"Meet Nash, Dawkins and Blatch," Lucas said.

He spread out three personnel folders each with a photograph stapled to the front. Lucas placed them in front of Larkin and watched the man glance down at the photos staring back at him.

Larkin had dark hair, a pockmarked face filled with deep crevices, with black eyes that were flat and lifeless. His skin tone was not good, as if he'd been on a recent drug binge, and he was thin. His appearance seemed to suggest that something was eating at him from the inside out.

But that was probably just Lucas's imagination.

Larkin did not wear anything remotely military. Instead, he had on blue jeans, a gray T-shirt and a black leather jacket.

As if he'd just arrived on his motorcycle.

"There's three of them?" Larkin asked. He raised an eyebrow as if he was receiving different information than he'd expected.

"It's a little more complicated than that," Lucas said as he picked up the phone to call Dr. Aldrich.

23

"Is this what you meant when you said that nothing happens out here and that I'd probably be bored out of my mind?" Pauling asked Tallon.

Bordeau had just left, and Pauling had taken her place in the living room across from Tallon.

He smiled. "Well, it has been boring, until you arrived. Maybe that's not a coincidence."

She laughed. ""Doubtful, but I appreciate the sentiment."

They sat in silence for a moment and then Pauling asked, "In all seriousness, what are you going to do?"

He shrugged. "Not much I really can do. I don't know anything about what happened."

Tallon snagged an iPad from the coffee table and swiped to the local news.

There was nothing reported.

"No story on the news yet," he offered.

"Well, I don't think she was making it up," Pauling said. "Had you ever met her before?"

"First time."

"She seems young for the gig."

"I vaguely remember something during election season about the job used to be her old man's," Tallon said. "I don't pay much attention to what's going on locally but I think her opponent made some sort of nepotism claim. Like she didn't deserve to be sheriff. But she won."

"Huh."

"Yeah, kind of odd there might have been a multiple homicide and no one's reported on it yet," Tallon said.

"I've still got some access leftover from days at the Bureau," Pauling offered. "Do you want me to do a little digging and see if anything's been posted?"

"Your first day here and I put you to work?" Tallon smiled. "You're going to think that was my plan all along."

"I always knew you were devious."

"If you want to take a quick peek, sure," he answered. "I'm kind of curious why she came to see me."

"Seems to me your reputation preceded you," Pauling pointed out.

"Maybe," Tallon said. "Or maybe she knows a lot more than she's letting on."

24

All Sheriff Bordeau knew at that moment was that she had a sick feeling inside. She'd been on patrol, heading back out to possibly interview anyone in the area of the homicide when she'd gotten a call from dispatch about a possible murder.

Even as she raced along the dirt highway toward the location of the scene, Bordeau had a strange feeling of déjà vu. This time, however, she wouldn't be so skeptical.

She spotted the motorhome on the side of the road, along with an ambulance, and an officer who'd already arrived.

Bordeau parked her squad car behind the other police vehicle, and the patrol officer approached her.

"The lady who called it in is over there," he said. "She's some kind of marathon runner or something. Didn't get too close. Said she could see it was something bad, called 9-1-1 and waited. I checked her out. She is who she says she is."

"Have you been inside?"

He nodded. "But I just looked, didn't touch a thing. Crime scene guys are on their way."

Bordeau already knew that but she didn't correct him. Instead, she went to the motorhome and went inside. The sight of so much blood told her she was right; without even seeing the victims she knew the person or persons who'd killed the four in the abandoned farmhouse had no doubt struck again.

Bordeau made her way down the center aisle of the vehicle, took in the blood splashed everywhere and the naked, mutilated woman hanging out of the back doorway. Beyond her, Bordeau could see a bedroom with bloody sheets.

She looked down at the dead body of the woman and knew it was the same handiwork of the killer who'd tortured the folks back at the abandoned farmhouse.

So much violence and death, she thought.

What the hell was she dealing with? she wondered.

The crime scene techs would arrive soon and Bordeau retraced her steps and waited outside the ambulance to interview the woman who'd called it in.

Bordeau thought back to her visit to Michael Tallon's place. Judging by the time of death, her best guess, he was probably in the clear on this one.

She wondered why the motorhome had pulled over. Or had the killer or killers already been inside.

What were they after?

Bordeau didn't know, but she had a feeling that unless she found some answers fast, this wasn't going to be the end of it.

25

Nash and Dawkins drove west, away from the sites of the first two operations, and while the terrain was less rugged, it was even more desolate, if that was possible.

Neither man spoke.

Dawkins seemed to be in a state of shock over the way Nash had killed Blatch. For his own self, Nash felt relieved that the constant struggle to control the red-haired freak was finally over.

No more rapes.

No more murdering of women.

No more Blatch.

Finally.

Dawkins turned on the radio and found a classic rock station. The band Free was saying it was *all right now*.

Hardly, Nash thought.

They were using the same four-wheel drive van they'd used to corral the motorhome, so Nash simply turned off from the road and bounced over several ravines, maneuvered behind a stand of rocks twenty feet tall and spotted a gulch created by water or wind that had winnowed between the two giant pieces of stone.

Nash parked the van and he and Dawkins exited, then met at the back. Nash threw open the doors to reveal Blatch's dead body.

They each took a leg and dragged the dead soldier to the gulch and tossed him in. He bounced and skittered along the edges, causing some stones to break free and roll down on top of him.

From the back of the vehicle, Dawkins grabbed a shovel and began to cover the body with sand and gravel.

Nash went toward the vehicle, then turned, quickly pivoted and shot Dawkins in the back of the head.

The force of the bullet carried the black man forward, where he landed in the gulch perpendicular to Blatch's body. Nash cocked his head, disappointed in the way Dawkins had landed, like a golfer not happy with where his chip had ended up on the green.

The gunshot echoed through the vast empty space and Nash stepped up to the gulch, took careful aim at Dawkins's head and fired until most of the dead man's head was blown to bits and the hammer clicked on an empty chamber.

Nash reached down, pulled Dawkins by the leg so his body was along the same line as Blatch's, then finished the job of burying them both.

"Next time try following orders," Nash told the dead men.

He'd murdered Blatch in a fit of anger but deep down, he knew he had to get rid of Dawkins, too. It was a shame, because of the two, Dawkins was the better soldier. But he could get out of control at times, too and now he'd seen his commanding officer murder a subordinate.

That wouldn't do in the long run.

So Nash had made the only decision he could.

He went to the back of the vehicle, tossed the shovel inside and got behind the wheel.

Nash reversed the van, took a different route to get back to the road, and then headed toward his command center.

He felt free at last from the incompetence of his men.

Now, he had to explain himself to the brass.

26

Pauling was amused by Tallon's home office. It was such a masculine space. A long, rectangular desk with a single office chair, flanked by a bank of video monitors on the right.

To the left was a printer, scanner, and a smaller desk stacked with papers and a disassembled shotgun.

There wasn't a single picture on the walls, or any other form of decoration. It was a workspace, and nothing more.

Pauling plugged in her laptop and used Tallon's secure Ethernet connection to launch her browser. It went directly into the FBI's violent offender database, via a back door Pauling's computer guy had installed. It technically wasn't an illegal breach, it was as if her access rights as an employee were never canceled.

With a few clicks of her mouse she quickly found an entry detailing the multiple homicide that had occurred in the area.

"Here it is," she said.

Tallon came into the office and hovered behind her, reading over her shoulder.

"Sounds nasty," he said.

They read in silence for several minutes.

"The victims were tortured, and the woman was most likely a victim of sexual assault," Tallon read.

"It was a family," Pauling noted.

"What?"

"Look at the supposed ages. A man and woman, both approximately thirty-five years old, and two juvenile males, around 14 and 16. A family. Maybe migrant workers. Illegals, perhaps?"

"Jesus," Tallon said. "And no weapons were found?"

"No, it doesn't look like they found any evidence the victims were anything but civilians."

"So why did Bordeau say it was a military operation?" Tallon wondered.

"I don't know why she came to talk to you, claiming soldiers may have been involved. I don't see a single piece of evidence that shows a connection with anything remotely military."

"The footprints," Tallon said. He had scanned down to image files that had been uploaded. "See those? Those tracks look like the kind of boots we used to wear in Afghanistan."

"That's it? That merited a visit? Someone could buy those at an army surplus store," Pauling pointed out.

He frowned at the images.

"What?" Pauling asked, seeing the confused expression on his face.

"That's really weird," he said, pointing at the descriptions written below the image. "All the footprints are the same size."

27

Lucas leaned back with detached amusement in his conference room chair and enjoyed the scene between Dr. Aldrich and Larkin.

It was a fascinating meeting between a brilliant, if slightly infamous scientist, and a cold stone contract killer.

Aldrich addressed Larkin with the same kind of tiresome condescension that he used with everyone and made obvious attempts to "dumb down" everything he said.

"Burton Nash," Aldrich said, pointing to the first of the photographs placed on the table by Lucas. "A highly decorated Marine with an extremely high level of commitment."

Larkin's soulless black eyes took in the image before him.

"Terry Dawkins," the doctor continued, pointing to the image of the black man. "Booted out of the Navy SEALs, spared a trial that would have brought a great deal of embarrassment to the service and to the country."

"Fun group you have here, Doc," Larkin said, his face completely devoid of humor.

"Finally, the worst of them," Aldrich continued, ignoring

Larkin. "Douglas Blatch. A highly competent soldier, and prodigious sex offender."

Larkin glanced down at the photo of Blatch. With his red hair he looked a little bit like Howdy Doody.

"How the hell did you let these three out into the world?"

"That's just it, we didn't," Lucas interjected. "Dawkins and Blatch are dead."

28

Bordeau pulled into the police station and spotted her Dad's civilian car – a red Hummer with vanity license plates that read THE LAW.

I'm going to have to talk to him, Bordeau thought. Hell, at this rate, he was spending more time in the office than she was. It was going to be hard to distance herself from the shadow of her father if he was constantly around.

Bordeau parked, went inside and stopped by the dispatcher to check the "in" basket by her name for priority cases.

There was a single, fairly thick folder waiting for her and she saw on its label that it was from the crime lab, no doubt the final report from the first homicide scene.

She went back to her office and was relieved to see that her father was nowhere around. Bordeau shrugged off her jacket and opened the file. She read through the information quickly at first, then went back a second time, lingering on the final piece of evidence that had been collected.

She was surprised that her own intuition had been wrong.

Because the last bit of evidence collected had been the only fingerprint not belonging to any of the victims.

It belonged to someone else.

Michael Tallon.

29

The dream was always the same.

In it, Nash was a young Marine sent on a mission to rescue some hostages in Afghanistan. Nash was the first one to enter the shabby hut at the outskirts of a village in the shadows of the towering, ominous mountains.

They were too late.

Everywhere was carnage. The men had been shot, execution-style, the women piled in a heap with most of their clothes gone, and the small dead children scattered about like discarded toys.

Nash stepped forward, toward the body of a young boy. As he got closer, he noticed that what he'd initially thought was blood on the boy's chest was actually writing.

Four letters.

Zotz.

His eyes snapped open and Nash realized he was having the same nightmare. And he was also pretty sure something had awakened him.

His hand found the semi-automatic pistol beneath the

T-shirt next to his bed on the floor. He swung his feet out of bed, stood, and silently crept into the hall.

It was the middle of the night.

Maybe he'd just imagined it.

There were all kinds of sound out here in the–

A hand clamped over Nash's mouth and a knife was put to his throat.

Nash was furious at himself for his carelessness. His mind raced, planning how he could talk his way out of the situation, maybe get to one of the several guns he'd stashed around the command center.

The gun was ripped from his grip and then he was whirled around to face his captor.

Or captors, actually.

Because standing before him were Dawkins and Blatch.

Alive and well.

And even in the dim light one fact was obvious.

Neither one even had a scratch on them.

30

"What do you mean they're dead?" Larkin asked. He was getting tired of the poor excuse of a man across the table from him. "I thought I was brought here to stop them from killing people."

"You are," Dr. Aldrich said. He had a smirk on his face that made Larkin want to punch him in the mouth.

"I guess I'm not understanding how they're killing people if they're already dead?" Larkin preferred the direct approach in everything he did and this was anything but. "What, did they leave a bomb somewhere?"

Dr. Aldrich took a deep breath but Lucas cut him off.

"Doctor, let's keep this as brief as possible," Lucas said. "We're losing operational hours as we speak."

Aldrich was clearly perturbed by the request but he took a moment before proceeding, ostensibly to condense what he had to say.

"I'm a clinical neurological researcher specializing in brain composition and immunological responses," he lectured Larkin. "You see, the brain is what is called a *privi-*

leged organ in the sense the body knows not to attack it. At least, not right away."

He paused and Larkin glanced over at Lucas, whose expression indicated he'd sat through the speech many times over.

"In fact, a researcher in China transplanted a brain into a monkey and the monkey lived for nine days. It was a huge breakthrough and provided the foundation for some of my early research."

He waved his hands in the air as if cigarette smoke was obscuring his vision. "But that's not what we're interested in," he continued. "Our focus is on partial brain transplant and rejuvenation. Almost like skin grafts, we can take small sections of one person's brain and graft it onto another. And since the brain is "privileged" the chance of the host brain rejecting the addition is quite low."

Larkin grimaced. "Let me guess, the army saw a way to weaponize this."

Dr. Aldrich smiled. "Of course they did. By taking the brains of highly skilled and specialized subjects, and grafting their key components onto the same host, the army hoped to create super soldiers."

"Why waste money on training?" Larkin said. "You can just slap together some extra pieces of brain, like rebuilding a car in a junkyard."

Lucas, who'd tilted his head back, laughed at the metaphor and how it so thoroughly impugned the importance of Dr. Aldrich's work. The doctor wouldn't care for that.

"A most inelegant way of summarizing my work," Aldrich responded.

Now Larkin was interested. "So whose brains did you snatch and who's the host?"

"Nash is the host," Lucas said. "He was brought in for surgery and nearly pronounced dead. We had already taken grafts from Dawkins and Blatch, two highly decorated soldiers, albeit with some issues of their own. However, we didn't have much to choose from and despite their drawbacks, we had to use them."

Larkin said, "Sounds to me like you're making excuses."

"No, but those issues, once implanted in Nash, began to blossom and become uncontrollable."

"So much so that Nash escaped, with the brains of two crazy killing machines stuck in his head?" Larkin asked.

Dr. Aldrich answered. "Again, your assessment is quite indelicate, but factually accurate."

"What's my objective?" Larkin asked.

"Bring back Nash and his 'friends,'" Lucas said, using air quotes to emphasize the word friends. "Preferably alive."

Larkin laughed and it was an unpleasant thing to witness, Lucas observed. Like watching a hyena lick his chops. "Yeah, bring him back *alive* with a couple of sociopaths bouncing around inside his skull?"

He let out a long breath.

"Probably not gonna happen."

31

D r. Aldrich studied Larkin, a disappointed look on his face.

Lucas had come close to dozing off, but Larkin was awake and extremely focused on the doctor.

"Are you shocked by what I've told you?" Aldrich asked his captive audience of one.

"Not at all," Larkin replied. "The army has been funding this kind of nonsense for years. I'm just surprised you believed your own bullshit and thought it would work."

The tone of Larkin's words roused Lucas from his stupor. He needed to take back control of both the conversation and the operation. Time was being wasted and somewhere out there chaos was unfolding.

"Okay, the important thing here is that we've taken some steps to make cleanup relatively neat," Lucas said.

"Like what?" Larkin said, his voice thick with skepticism.

"Let's just say that we've pointed the authorities in one direction, and it's the same direction that will hopefully lead the problem to its very own solution."

"What the hell are you talking about?" Larkin asked.

"I'm getting very tired of the lack of clarity. Are you guys confused or are you just trying to make it seem that way?"

Lucas sighed but inwardly admitted Larkin had a point so he cut to the chase. "We gave the cops the same name we gave Nash."

"I thought you said Nash was after some guy named Zotz."

"He is."

"So you gave the cops Zotz's name and then told Nash where to find him?"

"Not exactly," Lucas replied.

"There is no Zotz," Dr. Aldrich said. He'd been sitting silent for the past few minutes, waiting for something less operational and more in his area of expertise. "We invented him."

Larkin shifted in his seat. "Jesus, you people have been hopelessly ineffective but at least you've been busy, I'll give you that. "

Lucas had to be careful. He didn't want to anger one of the most lethal "exterminators" in the industry.

"It's really pretty simple," Lucas said.

"Prove it by showing me," Larkin shot back.

"Zotz isn't real," Aldrich reaffirmed. "We needed a target to set the experiment, or mission as you people call it, in motion."

Lucas stepped in. "So basically, we found someone to unwittingly become Zotz. He was an easy choice because he's ex-military, lives alone in the area, and has a highly secretive past. That way, the cops will be able to find him, but not before Nash does."

"And what's going to happen when Nash finds this guy?"

"Hopefully, they'll kill each other, but should one come

out of it alive, you're going to be there to make sure he doesn't stay that way."

"Let me guess," Larkin said. "And then I'm supposed to stage it so it looks like they were working together all along. And with both of them dead, it will be case closed."

"Excellent summary," Dr. Aldrich said, checking his watch and getting to his feet.

"So what's the name of the patsy we're going to claim is Zotz?"

Lucas slid a fourth picture across the table to Larkin.

"His name is Michael Tallon."

32

The gunshot was like rolling thunder in the dry riverbed less than a mile from Tallon's ranch.

He and Pauling were facing a row of paper targets on the other side of the wide swatch of dirt and stone. It was Tallon's homemade gun range and he used it often.

They were each firing Glock 17s and the match was even.

"Pretty impressive for an ex-Feebie," Tallon pointed out.

"You're not too shabby yourself," Pauling responded, happy that she was keeping pretty even pace with him. Then again, she wondered if he was keeping it competitive to be nice.

After a morning spent making love, they had talked about either going for a run or taking in some target practice. Since they'd just gotten finished with some exhausting exercise between the sheets, they'd decided on shooting practice instead of a long-distance trek.

As more shots ran throughout the empty space, Tallon considered upping the ante a bit. There was a target farther back–

"Tallon! Drop your weapon!"

He turned, saw Sheriff Bordeau standing behind him, her weapon drawn, with two other uniformed officers flanking her.

What the hell is it with this cop? he wondered. He was careful, though, because even though he knew he was innocent of whatever they were going to claim he'd done, he didn't want to get shot.

That was always a bad option.

Tallon slowly put down his gun and next to him, Pauling did the same.

"Hands up, get down on the ground."

He complied, and soon, he was handcuffed.

Lifted to his feet, the officers frisked him and found no other weapons.

"What's this about?" he asked.

Bordeau faced him.

"You're under arrest for murder."

33

The three of them sat together drinking beers and laughing.

"You actually tried to get rid of us," Dawkins said, his white teeth practically glowing, framed by his dark skin. "What were you thinking?"

The three of them were back in the command trailer, sitting around the table in the center of the kitchen, drinking beers. Nash hated to admit it, but he was glad they were all back together again.

He'd kind of missed his buddies.

"Bitch, we're here for the long haul," Blatch added. "And now that I know where your head's at, I'm going to keep my eye on you. However, I also feel like it's time to clear the air. I've got a thing for the ladies and don't ever try to get in my way again."

Blatch had picked up a pistol and was using it to accentuate his gestures. Now, he set it on the table, pointed directly at Nash.

Nash nodded to the voices in his head. They seemed real

to him, though, as if he was looking in a mirror and could see them over his shoulder.

"I learned my lesson," he said, in the empty trailer he'd been living in since he escaped the army base. To him, it was a command center, but in reality it was a rusty shell partially hidden beneath an outcropping of rock in the middle of the desert.

He finished his beer, walked over to the secure laptop he'd linked to a satellite server, encrypted so no one could use geotracking. He'd stolen the equipment on his escape from the army base.

Now, he tapped the screen and saw he had a new secure message.

Nash grabbed a fresh beer and double-clicked the message icon.

A photo filled his screen, and beneath it, an address.

Followed by one word.

Zotz.

34

I t took several hours of unproductive questioning for Sheriff Bordeau and her investigators to determine Pauling had nothing to do with the crimes. They also understood that interrogating a former FBI agent was no small task.

In other words, they knew they'd met their match.

When Bordeau entered the interview room and told Pauling she was free to go, Pauling made no sign to exit.

"On what basis did you make this arrest?" she asked Bordeau.

"I'm not at liberty to discuss details of an ongoing investigation," the sheriff responded. Pauling recognized the woman was in over her head, but at the same time, oddly confident. Which gave Pauling pause. What exactly was giving this sheriff such a strong conviction that Tallon had been involved in a murder. There was no other explanation for the arrest.

"Give me a break," Pauling said. "You have nothing. There was no evidence of Tallon at the crime scene. There was hardly any evidence at all."

Bordeau frowned at Pauling.

"You sound as if you've seen the evidence."

Pauling knew she was exposing that, but had decided to plow ahead anyway.

"One of your investigators told me what you found," she lied. "No DNA, no fibers, just some footprints that may or may not have been Army issue footwear. That's all you have to arrest Tallon? Once I have his attorney here, he'll be free in a matter of hours, you realize that, don't you? And then you'll have made yourself, and the sheriff's office liable for a whopper of a lawsuit."

Bordeau took a step back and Pauling knew she had the woman on the ropes. It wasn't a fair match. Pauling had decades of investigative experience, her time with the Bureau and her private practice to rely on.

The sheriff had slid into her current position based on her father's strings, probably. Maybe an incorrect assumption, but Pauling could tell the woman was out of her element. Probably not her fault. She actually seemed fairly bright, but a multiple homicide had not been on her radar.

"I'm not going to discuss our evidence with you," Bordeau finally said. "All I can tell you is you don't have the whole picture. Bring your lawyer."

"Have you double-checked the source of your information?" Pauling asked. "Chain of custody?"

"Of course I have," Bordeau snapped. "I told you you're free to go, so do I need to have you escorted from the building?"

Pauling got to her feet.

"The next time I see you, you're not going to be happy," Pauling said and walked out the door.

35

N ash knew a fortified compound when he saw it and the little adobe ranch complex fit the bill.

If ever there were signs of a military presence, this had it all. Nash could tell by the way the structure itself was laid out and the strategic placement of what little landscaping had been planted.

It was all about creating clear shooting lanes.

Zotz is here, Nash knew.

For defensive purposes, great care had been taken as well. It was nearly impossible to approach without being seen. Nash had also noticed at least two surveillance cameras, as well as what was most likely backup generator power and satellite linkages. He was also sure there were more surveillance devices hidden from view.

Zotz had planned well.

"What's the plan, chief?" Dawkins asked. He was impatient, and Nash could feel it in his head. They had left the van a mile back and hiked in. They all knew that everything that had happened before was just a buildup to now, the main event. This was what they had been planning and training for all this time. Their hard work was about to pay off.

Nash wanted Zotz's head on a stick, plain and simple.

"Yeah, what's the plan, I need some action," Blatch piped up. Nash saw Blatch's fiery red hair and blazing blue eyes in his mind. He knew the man's idea of action had nothing to do with getting Zotz, though. His interests were always more primal.

"Shut the hell up, you two," Nash said. "I need to think."

He turned the problem over in his mind, looked at both the challenge and the compound itself from every conceivable angle. Just when he was about to pick the least of the bad options available to him, he noticed a vehicle pull up to the driveway, key the garage door, and pull inside.

Nash had seen the driver.

A woman.

No sign of Zotz.

Was he already inside?

Or had Zotz sent a scout ahead?

Either way, Nash abandoned whatever plan he had in mind.

"Let's go," he said.

"Direct approach?" Dawkins asked, surprised.

"Its time to kick ass and don't bother with names," Nash answered. "The only name that's important is Zotz. Let's put down this bastard once and for all."

He started down from the rise.

Dawkins and Blatch were with him and they were locked and loaded, too.

36

From nearly a mile away, hidden in a thick stand of reddish boulders caught in the fading sun, Larkin watched Nash approach the house.

Larkin wondered what was going on in the poor son of a bitch's patch-worked brain. Three crazies ricocheting around the man's thought process. Larkin was surprised the guy could even walk.

It was interesting to see the soldier jogging toward the house, with no attempt at concealment.

Larkin knew why.

He, too, had been surprised to see a woman arrive alone to Tallon's house. Or "Zotz's" house as Nash believed it to be. The soldier had probably been assuming there would be an armed force defending Zotz. Instead, a lone woman drove up to the house and went inside.

At that point, all bets were off, Larkin knew.

He hoped for the sake of the mission that Tallon was already inside. If he wasn't, the "cleanup" plan Lucas had bragged about wouldn't work out so well. Instead, there'd be another dead woman, probably raped and tortured, and no one to pin the blame on because Larkin wouldn't be allowed to kill Nash. If he killed Nash and Tallon wasn't there, it would only make the police investigation continue.

And that would make Larkin's job tougher.

That was okay, though, he had to admit.

Usually, the messier the job, the higher it paid.

37

Pauling was glad the house had been turned back over to her after the investigators had performed their search. They had found nothing, she was sure. Once inside, she pondered what to do.

On the way back from the police station she'd already called her attorney and gotten a referral for the best criminal defense attorney money could buy who was getting on a plane in the next hour.

As she went about straightening and cleaning up what the cops had disturbed, her mind went over the sequence of events.

One thing particularly nagged at Pauling.

She knew Tallon hadn't killed those people.

So who had?

They had the wrong person in jail so the real killer was still out and about. Not a pleasant thought.

Plus, she'd seen the evidence on the FBI's database directly from the state crime lab. It should have been the exact same reports Bordeau had studied. So what had the sheriff seen to justify Tallon's arrest? Had she, Pauling, missed something? She knew she hadn't. Her background and attention to detail gave her the confidence to assert that nothing was missed. Especially something that would have caused someone to believe in Tallon's guilt.

No, something else was going on here.

Pauling had a bad feeling about the whole situation.

She ducked into Tallon's home office and went to the back of the room where he had one of his gun safes. They had opened it together in order to go to the range. Now, she saw that some of the guns had been taken by the sheriff's office.

All that was left were revolvers as they didn't shoot the right kind of ammunition that had been found at the crime scene, Pauling assumed. All of the more military-style assault rifles had been confiscated, probably for ballistics testing.

Pauling studied her choices and wondered if she really needed to arm herself. Was she overreacting?

Maybe. Maybe not.

She saw a Ruger Alaskan, which held a huge, powerful .44 Magnum round. Six of them to be exact. It was a big, heavy gun, but with a short barrel. She slid it off its peg and opened the cylinder to make sure it wasn't loaded.

At the bottom of the gun safe was a drawer containing ammunition. She found the box of .44 Magnum shells and loaded the gun, as well as two speed loaders Tallon had placed next to the powerful handgun's place on the rack.

Pauling slipped the speed loads into her pocket and was leaving the office when the bank of surveillance monitors caught her eye.

Because she'd just seen movement.

She focused on the screens.

Which one?

Pauling waited, listening for any sounds in the house.

There weren't any.

There.

A flash of a shoulder passing through the kitchen.

Pauling felt her heartbeat quicken.

Was it a cop who hadn't finished? Then why had she been told the house was clear?

She stepped tentatively into the hallway.

And heard voices.

It sounded like three people were arguing. A deep, baritone voice, a higher-pitched male voice, and then a shushing sound.

Pauling stepped into the kitchen and saw a man wearing army fatigues, carrying an automatic rifle. He was looking to his left, holding his finger to his lips in a *be quiet* gesture.

But there was no one there.

He turned back, saw Pauling and stopped. His rifle was pointed down, but Pauling had the big revolver in both hands, pointed directly at the intruder.

"Don't even think about it," she said to him.

In his eyes, Pauling could tell the man was calculating his options.

"Don't. You'll lose."

He acted like he didn't hear her.

"Where's Zotz?" he asked.

"Not here," Pauling answered. "Who are you?"

"Yeah, she's pretty, Blatch," the man said. "But you can't have her yet. Calm down."

Pauling thought it was an odd attempt to distract her. Making her think there was someone behind her?

"Put down your weapon," she said.

The man laughed and his voice changed to a higher

pitch. "Ooh, she's a tough one! This is totally turning me on."

The man's voice changed again.

"Tell us where Zotz is and you won't be harmed, I'll see to it."

Pauling studied the man. *Us?* She knew he was probably trying to distract her, use the empty threat that there were more people inside the house than just him.

"I'm not going to tell you again," she said. "Put it down. That's your last warning."

A deep baritone emerged from the man's mouth. "Bitch please," it said.

And then it changed again.

"Now, Dawkins!" the man in front of her said. He charged at her and Pauling fired the pistol.

A .44 Magnum is a huge round and the sound was like a cannon going off in the kitchen. The gun kicked so hard Pauling almost thought she'd lost control of the gun. It was like firing a hunting rifle one-handed.

The muzzle went straight up but Pauling used all of her hand strength to bring it back down because even though the first round had knocked the man backwards, he was somehow still on his feet and he hadn't dropped the rifle.

She fired again and the second round lifted him off his feet and he landed on his back.

Pauling whirled around, half expecting to see someone behind her.

There was no one.

She crossed the room to the dead man and picked up his rifle, then put her fingers against his throat.

He was dead.

The two rounds had made a mess of the man's chest,

blowing huge holes through and through. Blood gushed on Tallon's kitchen floor.

Pauling made her way through the rest of the house but there was no one. The man had either been bluffing or was completely unhinged as evidenced by the odd shift in voices.

She found her cell phone and called 9-1-1, telling them there'd been a shooting and to tell Sheriff Bordeau immediately.

When she hung up, she went back into the kitchen.

She went to the dead man and looked through his pockets. There was a wallet with an ID stating the dead man's name was Burton Nash.

Pauling had never heard of the man.

A quick search on her computer might help her find the right info–

The cold steel of a gun barrel placed against the back of her neck made her go cold.

"Drop the gun," a voice said.

Pauling set down the big revolver as well as Nash's ID. She slowly turned and saw a thin man with black hair, pale, pockmarked skin and a face full of deep lines.

He was only a few feet away and he was smiling at her with teeth that were sharp and pointy.

Feral.

"You got the three for the price of one," he said.

38

"Where's Tallon?" the man asked.

"Who are you?"

"My name's Larkin, not that it matters. Who the hell are you?"

"Pauling, not that it matters."

Larkin pointed at the dead man.

"Where's Tallon?" he repeated.

"Jail."

"That's unfortunate."

The man glanced behind Pauling at the dead man on the floor. "Jeez, what'd you shoot him with, a cannon?"

She didn't answer, instead, she asked, "What did you mean when you said it was three for the price of one?"

"Ah, one of those Alaskan revolvers," the man replied, seeing the big handgun next to the dead body. "What is that, a .44 Mag? Impressive. Powerful enough to kill a grizzly bear or three people at once," he said again, laughing.

Pauling wondered what he meant and he must have seen the confusion in her eyes.

"Your new friend there had multiple personalities,"

Larkin said. "Another one of those brilliant ideas by some lunatic back at the Pentagon. A super soldier with the brain of three men." He glanced down again at the dead man. "Yeah, didn't seem to work out too well."

Now she understood, and saw how this had landed on Tallon's doorstep.

"It looks like the easy cleanup I'd been promised ain't gonna happen," Larkin said. "At least not as far as Tallon is concerned. I'm going to have to walk away from this one for a bit. I've always said any operation is a good one, if you can walk away afterward."

The pistol in his hand was a small caliber automatic, with a compact but sturdy sound suppressor at the end of it.

He began to raise it when a voice from behind him called out.

"Drop the gun!"

Larkin smiled. He didn't drop the gun but instead, slowly turned to face the voice he seemed to recognize, keeping Pauling in his line of vision.

"Ah, Sheriff Bordeau to the rescue," he said. "Look, this is above your pay grade, you're going to need to–"

A shot rang out and Larkin took a step back. He seemed shocked that the young woman had fired.

He tried to raise his weapon as another round was fired. It crashed into the ceiling above Larkin's head as Pauling dove for her revolver.

Pauling knew the young sheriff had panicked, shot too soon, and was now firing blindly.

Pauling came up with the big revolver as Larkin was staggering to the side, trying to raise his automatic.

To her right, Pauling saw that Bordeau was frozen, and the gun in her hand was shaking.

Pauling brought the big revolver in line and shot the

dark-haired man in the temple, the huge bullet crashing into his skull and spraying brain, blood and bone all over Tallon's kitchen cabinets.

He crashed sideways into the wall and slid down to the floor, leaving a blood smear marking his descent.

Pauling carefully set down the revolver and faced Sheriff Bordeau. The last thing she wanted was to get shot now by a nervous cop.

"How'd you get here so fast?" Pauling asked her. "And please, lower your gun."

Sheriff Bordeau holstered her weapon. Her pretty face was pale and she was out of breath, no doubt shocked she had just shot a man and probably unnerved by a second dead man behind Pauling.

"I was already on my way when you called 9-1-1," Bordeau answered, her voice shaky.

"Why?"

"I think I know how that evidence against Tallon was planted."

Pauling nodded. She looked around at the carnage in the kitchen.

Some guest I am, she thought. *My second day here and look at what a mess I've made.*

39

L ucas roused Dr. Aldrich from his sleep.

"Emergency, Dr. You're needed in DC as soon as possible."

Aldrich sat up in his bed. He had been assigned a private room, separate from the enlisted barracks. The room had a single bed, a desk and a dresser.

"You're kidding me," he said. "What about Nash?"

"Nash has been taken care of and the project has been reassigned to DC, which is why you're being put on the first flight out."

Dr. Aldrich got to his feet. "What do you mean Nash has been taken care of? If he's not alive, I'm going to have you and your boss Crawford reassigned to Siberia."

"Not sure we have a base in Siberia, but I appreciate the thought," Lucas replied evenly. "I'll meet you out front in five minutes."

Aldrich began to dress. "At least I'll finally get out of this desert hellhole."

Five minutes later, the doctor was climbing into the back

seat of an army truck with a single, small travel bag. Two uniformed soldiers were in the front of the vehicle.

Lucas waved goodbye as they drove and then he turned to his commanding officer, Crawford. The grizzled face showed no sign of relief or humor. He was all business as usual.

He turned to Lucas. "It's only a matter of time before the Feds show up. I hope you gave specific instructions on where the doctor should be relocated."

Lucas nodded.

"I told them that when they thought the grave was deep enough, dig down another twenty feet."

40

Bordeau found her father where she knew she would; seated in front of the big fireplace. A roaring fire was going and he had a glass of whiskey in his big, meaty paw.

Somewhere in the kitchen, her mother was making dinner.

Bordeau wouldn't be staying for the meal.

"I hope you've got yourself a good lawyer," she told her father.

"What are you talking about?" he glowered at her.

"You've got four murders in the first killing, two in the second, plus a bartender near the army base, and now two more dead people."

"I wasn't near any of 'em. Had nothing to do with it."

The big man sipped his whiskey and stared into the fire. A log popped and a shower of sparks briefly lit up the old man's face.

Bordeau stood in front of her father, her feet spread wide, refusing to be ignored or discounted.

"When I got to the station and found the evidence file," she said, "there was a fingerprint from Tallon supposedly found at the crime scene. But the original evidence for the crime lab showed no such thing. I only discovered it because Tallon's friend Pauling said she had seen the original file. I'm assuming whoever planted the print in the file was planning on adding it to the original, digital report but things moved too quickly. But I had to ask myself, how did that print end up in my file first?"

"No idea what you're talking about, girl," he said. He looked past her, over her shoulder to the kitchen and called out to his wife. "Jenny, when is that chili going to be done?" he shouted. "I'm hungry."

"This was a military operation, through and through," Bordeau said. "You've always been on great terms with the boys out at that base. Your buddies, even. A bunch of good ol' boys, right? If they needed someone locally to steer the investigation a certain way, you'd be the perfect candidate. In fact, I saw your truck at the station the same day I got the doctored evidence file."

"Coincidence," he said, draining the last of the whiskey from his glass.

Bordeau gave him a patronizing smile.

"You'd better hope so. Because Tallon's girlfriend is a former FBI agent and she's got them involved now. They'll be going out to the army base and probably arresting some folks, who will eventually spill their guts to avoid military prison. It'd sure be a shame if your retirement home was a federal slammer, Daddy."

He looked at her for the first time, anger flashing in his eyes.

"Anything else you got to say on your way out?"

"Yeah," she countered. "Between now and your sentencing, don't ever set foot in my police station again."

Bordeau slammed the door shut behind her.

41

"What was that you were saying about how boring it was out here?" Pauling asked Tallon. He'd been back home now for less than twenty-four hours but they'd already made love twice. They were still in bed and Pauling was basking in the heat from Tallon's body.

"Post-prison sex is awesome," he said. "All that time in the joint really gets a man wound up, if you know what I mean."

"You weren't even in jail that long," Pauling said.

"Long enough, believe me."

The crime scene technicians had already hauled the bodies away and Pauling had arranged for a crew specializing in hazardous cleanup to take care of the rest.

"Now what?" she asked him.

He sighed, ran his hand along her firm, naked hip. He loved the sound of her raspy voice.

"I don't know," he said. "I'm in no hurry to see what sunup brings. Kinda happy to just be where I am right now."

Pauling wrapped her arms and legs around him.
"Me too," she said.

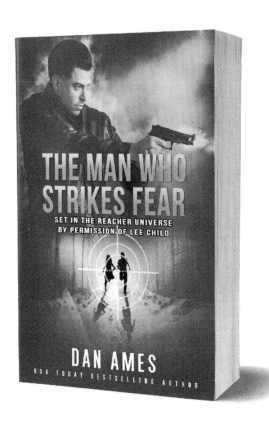

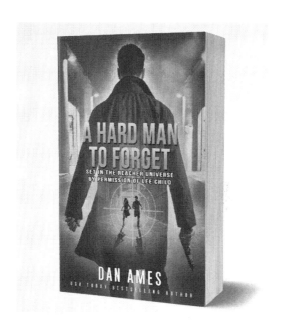

Book One in The JACK REACHER Cases

BOOK ONE IN A THRILLING NEW SERIES

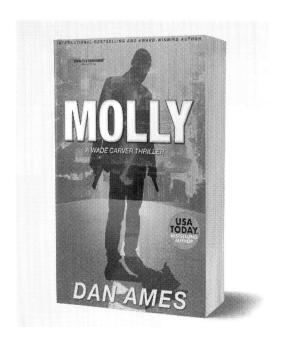

A Blazing Hot New Mystery Thriller Series!

ALSO BY DAN AMES

The JACK REACHER Cases #1 (A Hard Man To Forget)

The JACK REACHER Cases #2 (The Right Man For Revenge)

The JACK REACHER Cases #3 (A Man Made For Killing)

The JACK REACHER Cases #4 (The Last Man To Murder)

The JACK REACHER Cases #5 (The Man With No Mercy)

The JACK REACHER Cases #6 (A Man Out For Blood)

The Jack Reacher Cases #7 (A Man Beyond The Law)

The JACK REACHER Cases #8 (The Man Who Walks Away)

DEAD WOOD (John Rockne Mystery #1)

HARD ROCK (John Rockne Mystery #2)

COLD JADE (John Rockne Mystery #3)

LONG SHOT (John Rockne Mystery #4)

EASY PREY (John Rockne Mystery #5)

BODY BLOW (John Rockne Mystery #6)

MOLLY (Wade Carver Thriller #1)

SUGAR (Wade Carver Thriller #2)

ANGEL (Wade Carver Thriller #3)

THE KILLING LEAGUE (Wallace Mack Thriller #1)

THE MURDER STORE (Wallace Mack Thriller #2)

FINDERS KILLERS (Wallace Mack Thriller #3)

DEATH BY SARCASM (Mary Cooper Mystery #1)

MURDER WITH SARCASTIC INTENT (Mary Cooper Mystery #2)

GROSS SARCASTIC HOMICIDE (Mary Cooper Mystery #3)

KILLER GROOVE (Rockne & Cooper Mystery #1)

BEER MONEY (Burr Ashland Mystery #1)

THE CIRCUIT RIDER (Circuit Rider #1)

KILLER'S DRAW (Circuit Rider #2)

TO FIND A MOUNTAIN (A WWII Thriller)

STANDALONE THRILLERS:

THE RECRUITER

KILLING THE RAT

HEAD SHOT

THE BUTCHER

BOX SETS:

AMES TO KILL

GROSSE POINTE PULP

GROSSE POINTE PULP 2

TOTAL SARCASM

WALLACE MACK THRILLER COLLECTION

SHORT STORIES:

THE GARBAGE COLLECTOR

BULLET RIVER

SCHOOL GIRL

HANGING CURVE

SCALE OF JUSTICE

ABOUT THE AUTHOR

Dan Ames is a USA TODAY Bestselling Author, Amazon Kindle #1 bestseller and winner of the Independent Book Award for Crime Fiction.

www.authordanames.com
dan@authordanames.com

18106951R00076

Printed in Great Britain
by Amazon